Walter Crane, Edmund Evans

This Little Pig, his Picture Book

Containing, This Little Pig, the Fairy Ship, King Luckieboy

Walter Crane, Edmund Evans

This Little Pig, his Picture Book
Containing, This Little Pig, the Fairy Ship, King Luckieboy

ISBN/EAN: 9783744650984

Printed in Europe, USA, Canada, Australia, Japan

Cover: Foto ©Andreas Hilbeck / pixelio.de

More available books at **www.hansebooks.com**

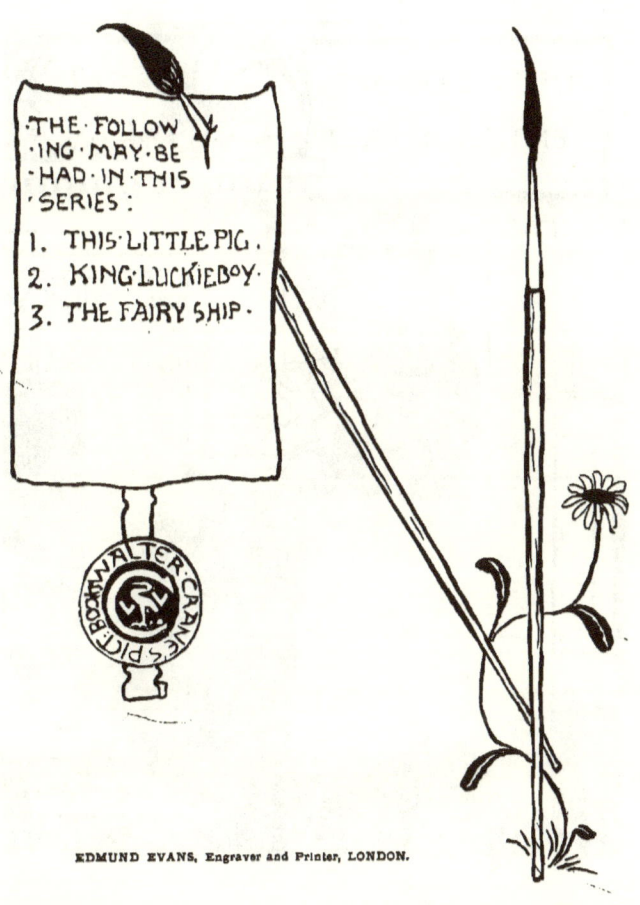

·THE·FOLLOW
·ING·MAY·BE
·HAD·IN·THIS
·SERIES:

1. THIS·LITTLE·PIG.

2. KING·LUCKIEBOY·

3. THE FAIRY SHIP·

WALTER CRANE'S PICT BOOK

EDMUND EVANS, Engraver and Printer, LONDON.

: THIS LITTLE PIG :
WENT TO MARKET

: THIS LITTLE PIG :

WENT TO MARKET

:THIS LITTLE PIG:

:STAYED AT HOME:

THIS
LITTLE
PIG
HAD
ROAST
BEEF

4

:HOME:

www.ingramcontent.com/pod-product-compliance
Lightning Source LLC
Chambersburg PA
CBHW020627260626
47157CB00009B/3207

* 9 7 8 3 7 4 4 6 5 0 9 8 4 *